by

W. NIKOLA-LISA

illustrated by

JESSICA CLERK

DUTTON CHILDREN'S BOOKS · NEW YORK

Tangletalk *was inspired by several lines of verse I found in Peter and Iona Opie's book,* The Lore and Language of Schoolchildren *(Oxford, 1959). Although the original verse was set in Liverpool, England, where the Opies collected the sample, I chose to locate the tale in Boston largely because I had recently visited the city and found its ambience compatible with its English counterpart.*

W.N.L.

Library of Congress Cataloging-in-Publication Data
Nikola-Lisa, W. Tangletalk / by W. Nikola-Lisa; illustrated by Jessica Clerk.
—1st ed. p. cm.
Summary: Recounts some of the strange upside-down events that happened in "the month of Boston, In the wonderful city of May."
ISBN 0-525-45399-7
[1. Stories in rhyme. 2. Humorous stories.] I. Clerk, Jessica, ill. II. Title.
PZ8.3.N5664Tan 1997 [E]—dc20 96-24548 CIP AC
Published in the United States 1997 by Dutton Children's Books,
a division of Penguin Books USA Inc.
375 Hudson Street, New York, New York 10014
Designed by Sara Reynolds
Printed in Hong Kong
First Edition
1 3 5 7 9 10 8 6 4 2

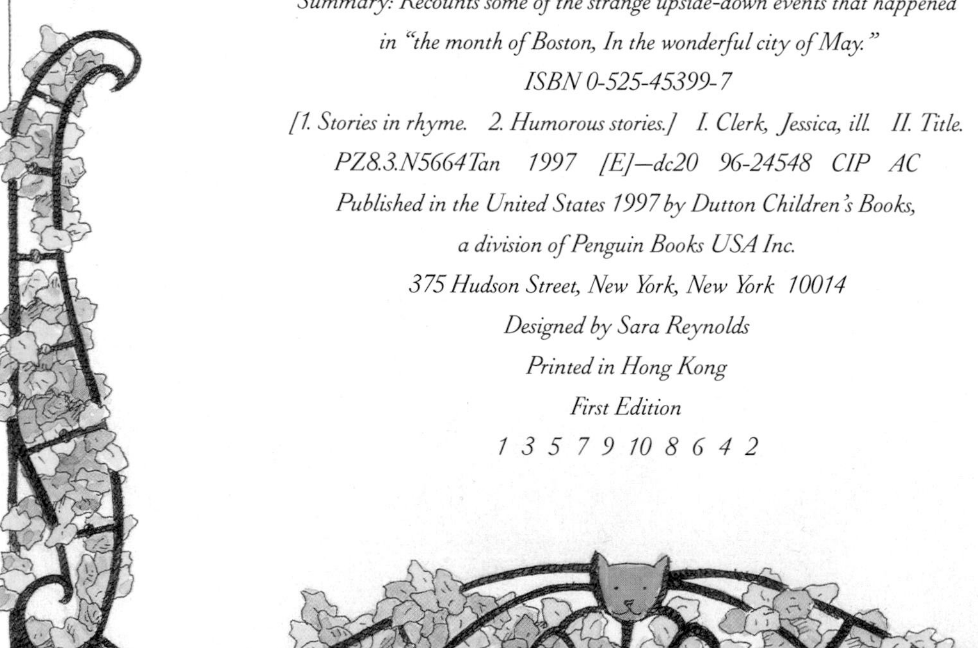

TO NADIA TORMEL AND THE GIZ—W.N.L.
FOR TOM—J.C.

'Twas in the month of Boston,
In the wonderful city of May,

The snow was raining wildly,
The streets were dry and gay.

The flowers were singing sweetly.
The birds were in full bloom.

My cat was in the basement,
Sweeping the upstairs room.

A mouse flew by my window.
Butterflies nibbled cheese.

My canary swam in circles
While the goldfish chirped in the breeze.

In a pot, my socks were simmering.
Lunch was pinned to the line.

My chair dashed up the chimney
When I sat down to dine.

At the corner an onion cleared tables.
Two cucumbers scraped the grill.

The sink chased a load of dishes
Out the door and up the hill.
TANGLE

A cabbie cooed and cackled
While three pigeons drove his car.

AND FINE PIPES
CIGARS
CAFE
A fireman watched in wonder
As rats doused a huge cigar.

In the park, policemen hid acorns
While squirrels paraded by.

A nanny taking a birdbath
Saw a duck teach her baby to fly.

An ice-cream cart sailed on the wind,
Spilling double-scoop, autumn-leaf cones.

An organ-grinder danced on his hands
While his monkey piped merry old tunes.

To escape this upside-down world,
I ran home at a galloping walk.

Tonight I would sleep in the kitchen—
Let tomorrow untangle my talk.

Oh, 'twas in the month of Boston,
In the wonderful city of May,
The snow was raining wildly,
The streets were dry and gay.